Jeremy Goes to Camp Good Grief

Rebecca DiSunno

Sarah Zimmerman

Priscilla Ruffin

Illustrations by Karin Ralph

An East End Hospice Bereavement Program Publication

East End Hospice, Westhampton Beach, NY

Acknowledgements

This book, and Camp Good Grief itself, would not be possible without the extraordinary support and encouragement of the East End Hospice Board of Directors. We extend our gratefulness to each member of the Board.

There is no fee for participation in Camp Good Grief. The Camp is underwritten by proceeds from the East End Hospice Thrift Shop, by grants and generous donations from the East End community, and by the caring efforts of the East Hampton Rotary – which donates delicious lunches for Campers, and whose members prepare and serve lunch and clean everything up afterwards! Very special acknowledgment is made to Sue Kohl Katz, whose devotion to our work led her to found the Valentine Salon - an event to raise funds for Camp Good Grief that continues on in her memory.

We thank the Camp therapists, each superbly talented, who freely give their skills to ensure that every child receives only their best effort . . . our Camp nurse who gives up her vacation to see to the needs of the children . . . our volunteer coordinator for guiding her volunteers to give their time and talent for the children, and the young volunteers themselves who hold sock hops, talent shows, and bake sales to raise funds, and the teen volunteers who give up summer jobs to be a part of Camp . . . the gifted friends who volunteer each year for Camp, many since its inception . . . St. Gabriel's Youth Retreat Center, for allowing us the use of their beautiful site; the serene beauty of St. Gabriel's on Shelter Island is the most perfect place to hold Camp Good Grief . . . the people and businesses across our communities who have given so generously over the years to benefit the children . . . our extraordinary support staff who leave no stone unturned in the quest to make each year at Camp better than the one before . . . and the artists, editor, designer, and printer who offered their devotion to this work.

And most of all we thank you . . . the families who at a most tender time entrust us to care for your children.

© 2004 by East End Hospice, Inc.

Illustrations © 2004 by Karin Ralph

481 Westhampton-Riverhead Road ▪ PO Box 1048 ▪ Westhampton Beach, NY 11978 ▪ www.eeh.org

First Edition June 2004 ▪ All rights reserved

Editing & Production by Terry Walton ▪ Design by Inger Gibb ▪ Printed by AvonPress

Library of Congress Control Number: 2004106685 ▪ ISBN 0-9754932-0-5

Suggested citation:

DiSunno, R., Zimmerman, S., & Ruffin, P. (2004) *Jeremy Goes to Camp Good Grief.*
Westhampton Beach, NY: EAST END HOSPICE

Dedication

Dedicated to the children who bravely share their stories
of love and loss . . . and without whose vitality and natural grace this
book could not have been written.

About Camp Good Grief

Camp Good Grief is a summer day camp for children who have experienced a loss. It was founded in 1997 by East End Hospice, Inc., in Westhampton Beach, NY. In the five-day camp experience, children of all ages gather together with a single purpose. For a concentrated period of time and under the guidance of skilled therapists who use the proven techniques of play therapy, art therapy, and group therapy, the children gain proficiency in managing the painful and confusing feelings that are associated with grief and loss.

The work of Camp Good Grief and the writing of this book make valuable contributions to the study of children's bereavement. Camp Good Grief is based on an interdisciplinary approach to the treatment of children's grief. Theoretical frameworks from the disciplines of psychiatry, social work, art therapy, nursing, child development, parenting, and psychology are the basis for the design of this innovative children's bereavement program, Camp Good Grief.

For Parents and Caregivers . . .

This book is written for children who have experienced the death of someone they love. It is the story of a child, Jeremy, and his new friends as they spend a week at a bereavement camp called Camp Good Grief. As the week progresses, Jeremy learns to give words to his feelings of grief. He begins to understand how the loss has changed his family, and, with his new friends, to understand that he is not alone in his grief.

This book is helpful for those who are caring for a grieving child. During emotionally charged times such as those following the death of a family member, friend, or teacher, children need us to understand what they are thinking and feeling. As this story of Jeremy is written, it will give to parents, grandparents, teachers, therapists, and caregivers new insight and a deeper appreciation of a grieving child's thoughts and feelings.

We believe that children reading Jeremy's story and attending Camp Good Grief will be helped to find the language and confidence needed to recognize painful feelings, and express them to those who are caring for them.

It is our sincere hope that by reading Jeremy's story and attending Camp Good Grief, your children will acquire a model for coping with loss that they may apply throughout their lifetime. Reading this book with your children will help your family to talk about the death, to share feelings of loss and grief, to comfort one other as you face the challenges ahead.

Rebecca DiSunno, RNCS, MA-ATR-BC, PhD, Art Therapist
Sarah Zimmerman, R-ACSW, Bereavement Coordinator, East End Hospice
Priscilla Ruffin, RN, MS, CS, NPP, Director, East End Hospice

Jeremy didn't want to get out of bed. Thoughts of the first day of camp were worrying him. Jeremy just lay there thinking, "I've never been to camp. Tommy said camp food is disgusting! And, bugs . . . I hate bugs now. That's it! I'm not going! If Mom were here she wouldn't make me go. But then, that's why they want me to go . . . because of MOM."

Jeremy didn't want to think about his mom right now. "Everything has changed," he said to his furry cat Shazaam.

1

He tried to remember what his dad had said about Camp Good Grief. "Well, one good thing is, I get to go on a ferry . . . a boat that takes cars on it," he said to himself. "And, there are other kids. Kids whose mom wouldn't make them go either if she. . . . Who's going to take care of me? Oh, I don't know about this." Jeremy jumped out of bed and ran downstairs in tears, pleading, "Dad, couldn't I just stay with you today?"

Jeremy's dad was making breakfast. He still couldn't get used to how

many things there were to do in the morning, getting Tommy and Jeremy ready for the day and himself off to work. He was feeling pretty sad and now, with Jeremy screaming, everything was chaos. . . .

In the car on the way to the ferry, Jeremy was still feeling very unhappy. He continued to yell, "No one ever listens to me anymore. I told you, I *hate* scrambled eggs! Now I have a stomachache! Dad, you never remember anything!" Jeremy folded his arms across his chest and scowled.

J eremy and his dad arrived at the ferry stop. Jeremy got out of the car very slowly and sat on a big rock next to his dad. A pretty girl about Tommy's age walked over to them, carrying a clipboard. She had long blond hair and was wearing a tan shirt with CAMP GOOD GRIEF on the front of it. "Hi, my name is Katie," she said, smiling right at Jeremy.

Jeremy looked up cautiously. A boy about Jeremy's size, dark haired and wearing a NY Yankees baseball cap, was standing near her, quietly giving Jeremy the once-over. Katie explained she was there to help new kids coming to camp. She had been a new camper herself three years ago, and now she was a youth volunteer.

All of a sudden a great-looking hot red convertible pulled up right in front of them. Katie called out "Hi, Bill!"

Bill was all smiles as he turned off the music and got out of his car. He was wearing a shirt just like Katie's. He told the kids he was a Hospice volunteer, and he'd be taking them to and from Camp Good Grief each day as well as doing lots of activities with them. Bill asked the kids if they'd like to ride with him to camp.

Jeremy couldn't believe it! He looked at his dad, hoping he'd approve. Jeremy's dad looked pleased and said, "What a great car! Be sure to fasten your seat belts!" Jeremy said good-bye to his dad. He and Katie, the kid with baseball cap, and two other kids named Brad and Sue got into the shiny red convertible, buckled up, and zoom, zoom! Off they went.

The ferry ride was fun, Jeremy decided. The red car, the new kids, it all seemed kind of adventurous. And, they were going to an *island!*

By the time they reached camp Jeremy knew that Brad, Sue, and the kid with the baseball cap were new campers too, and that Katie was fourteen years old and really had been to camp three times. Jeremy wondered who'd ever want to go to camp three times. *Three times?* What kind of a place was this?

Jeremy looked around. He was surprised to see humungous tents at the bottom of a grassy hill, overlooking the water. Green lawns and big shady trees surrounded everything. It looked like a big party. Something was happening everywhere!

He could see sailboats out on the bay and a swimming pool right near shore. Some boys were kicking a soccer ball out on the grass below the hill. The kid with the baseball cap looked at Jeremy and smiled. He had been silent all the way to camp, but Jeremy had the feeling he had a secret he wanted to share.

9

Katie introduced Jeremy and the kid with the baseball cap to a friendly grown-up named Anne. As they were talking, Jeremy learned his new friend's name . . . Davey. Anne gave Davey and Jeremy each a backpack. Inside, Jeremy found a blue camp shirt, a camp hat, and sunscreen. Davey had the same blue shirt inside his backpack.

As the boys pulled on their camp shirts, Anne asked them to put on some sunscreen - it was a very hot, sunny day. Jeremy dabbed on the lotion, remembering how his mom used to rub sunscreen all over him, even on his toes! Jeremy smiled, and began to feel a bit better inside and out.

Just then a whistle blew. Anne, Jeremy, Davey, and five other kids all went over to join a large circle with the other campers. Katie and the other youth volunteers and grownups were there too. Everyone was wearing CAMP GOOD GRIEF shirts in lots of different colors - blue, red, yellow, lime, tan, orange, pink, periwinkle, purple, aqua, and olive. The colors seemed to go with the

kids' ages. Jeremy's group all wore blue.

Peggy, who was wearing an orange camp shirt, began playing the guitar. They all joined hands and began to sing this song:

I am fine at
Camp Good Grief,
I am fine all day.
I am fine if I'm
laughin' or I'm cryin' –
I know I'm fine at
Camp Good Grief . . .

13

14

Jeremy watched. Standing in a circle? Singing songs? But after a bit he decided, "Well, I kind of like it." Everyone else seemed to like it too. So he joined in. . . .

All that day Jeremy and Davey went to camp activities together – arts & crafts, art therapy, sports & games, serious talks in "small group," even searching for things along the beach. Davey didn't talk much but Jeremy learned a lot about both Davey and himself that first day.

During art therapy, Jeremy sat with three other boys at a small table. Linda, the art therapist, handed out clay as she spoke quietly to the group. "All of us here at camp have had someone we love die," she said. Jeremy looked around at the other boys at his table. "So these guys had the same thing happen to them," he realized. . . .

Linda described how memories help kids - and adults too - with the difficult feelings that everyone has about death. She talked some more about memories, and how they help keep the person in our hearts. Then she asked all the kids to take the clay and "make a memory" about the person who died.

Everyone began pounding and slapping the clay. Really loud thumps and whacks - the noise was amazing! The clay began to feel warmer as Jeremy pounded and pounded. One

boy asked Jeremy what he was going to make. Jeremy had been thinking how much he *used to* like to hunt for bugs . . . before his mom died. But he didn't want to make a bug out of the clay. So he took a chance and told this to the group at his table. Everyone just listened. . . .

Another boy told a story about how he liked to go fishing with his dad, and how they would always laugh when they caught spider crabs instead of fish. A third boy said he would like to know what heaven looked like, because everyone kept telling him that was where his older brother was. Jeremy had wondered about heaven too. Did it really exist? The other kids began to tell what they knew about heaven. It seemed everyone told about heaven except Davey. Davey listened and quietly worked on his clay.

After a while Jeremy looked over at Davey's clay. "Gee, Davey, that looks like a staircase!" he said. Davey's eyes seemed to light up. One of the other boys looked at Davey's work and exclaimed, "Hey! If we all put our clay together we could make a giant staircase!"

This sounded like a great idea to Jeremy. "I'm in," he said, adding his clay to the pile that was beginning to become a

huge lump. Someone said, "It'll be a staircase to heaven!" The boys got to work.

Later in art therapy, the kids were invited to talk about their clay pieces and their memories. Jeremy felt very proud of his group and their beautiful staircase. When he thought of his mom being in heaven, he realized that the funny feeling in his throat had gone away.

At the end of the day, Jeremy and Davey walked over to join a special activity under the big tent. Kids were making their own ice cream sundaes! Katie was helping to serve the ice cream. Vanilla, chocolate, and strawberry - plus chocolate sprinkles, M&M's, Gummy Bears, rainbow sprinkles, Reese's Pieces, cookie crumbs, chocolate sauce, butterscotch sauce, strawberry sauce, and whipped cream and cherries. "Cool!" Jeremy said. "I'm coming back here tomorrow!"

The next morning Jeremy's dad was shocked. Just as he was about to call Jeremy to come to breakfast, Jeremy came running down the stairs - all dressed with his blue camp shirt on, and his hair combed. What had gotten into Jeremy? Dad decided not to ask any questions.

This time on their way to the ferry, Jeremy was humming a tune. His dad looked over and smiled. Jeremy wondered out loud if Davey would be at the ferry. When his dad stopped the car, there was Davey in his blue camp shirt with his NY Yankees baseball cap. Jeremy said "Bye, Dad," and jumped out of the car. He and Davey soon found Katie, Sue, and Brad. They climbed into Bill's car. Jeremy waved goodbye to his dad and they headed off together for the day.

The ferry ride was as much fun as the day before. At camp, Jeremy and Davey ran over to the art room to check on their clay staircase. There it was, sitting in the center of a large table with lots of other clay pieces surrounding it. It was safe. As they heard the whistle blow the boys hustled off to meet the rest of their blue shirt group. This time, when they circled around for the camp song Jeremy and Davey stood side by side holding hands like everybody else.

Today, again, they gathered in small group with Anne. Anne asked each child if they would fill in the blanks to the sentence, "When _____ died, I felt _____." As the campers each took a turn to speak Anne handed them a big white Teddy Bear to hold. It was the first time Jeremy had ever said out loud that when his mom died he felt **afraid!** Sue shared that she felt so **lonely** after her grandmother died. Brad shared that he felt **angry** with all adults after his baby sister died. Another boy shared that he felt **confused** when his dad died.

Davey didn't share anything. One of the boys said, "Hey Davey, why can't you tell us about your feelings? We all told you!" Jeremy was feeling bad for Davey. Sue spoke up, "He doesn't have to talk. Just look at his face and you can tell what he's thinking." Jeremy looked at Davey. "She's right," he thought. Davey looked as though he felt **afraid, lonely, angry, confused,** and **sad,** all at the same time.

Next, Anne asked the campers to tear a paper heart in half. She asked them to write on the torn pieces what it

felt like to have a broken heart. Then they taped the two pieces together, and wrote on the back what they thought they might need to mend their broken hearts. Jeremy wrote *I need friends that understand*. When he peeked at Davey's, he saw that on the back of his heart, Davey had carefully drawn a smiling face

with an open mouth and great big ears. Was that what Davey needed to mend *his* broken heart?

That afternoon in arts and crafts, sitting at long tables under one of the tents, Jeremy learned how to make a beaded alligator key chain. He liked it so much that he made a bright red one for his brother Tommy. Later, when the camp gathered for a special event, Jeremy was excited to see that a magician was going to do a show! Magic was one of Jeremy's favorite things. . . .

He watched the tricks carefully. At the end of the show
the magician gave everyone a magic wand. Jeremy was excited,
this gave him an idea! . . . Bill, the Hospice volunteer, had been
asking all the kids what they could do in a Talent Show on the
last day of camp. Jeremy whispered his idea to Davey. Davey
nodded his head in agreement. The boys gave each other
high fives. They headed over to join the circle for the camp
song, then off to the ferry for the ride home.

Wednesday, the third day of camp, dawned hot and sunny. Jeremy hunted around his room for his camp shirt, and remembered he needed his swimsuit today too. Luckily, a slightly damp one was still on the floor near his closet. He grabbed it and stuffed it into his backpack. When he found his shirt, under his bed, it was rumpled and all covered with fur. Shazaam had been sleeping on it. It was still warm. He pulled the shirt over his head. It sure smelled funny. Jeremy thought to himself that his clothes didn't smell the same, and nothing was the same, now that Mom was gone.

At camp that morning, some kids were playing a game of kickball. Jeremy looked around for Davey, but didn't see him. Alone, he grabbed a soccer ball and kicked it for a while before the whistle blew for the camp song. By now, Jeremy knew all the words. Sometimes at night the song kept going round and round in his head –

"I am fine at Camp Good Grief,
I am fine all day . . ."

The blue group went to art therapy first today. Jeremy was glad he was going to make something in art, but he was feeling a little grumpy and didn't really know why. In the art room he chose to sit next to Sue. Davey was sitting with Brad and a few other boys, and smiled over at him. All the kids had what the art therapist called "diorama boxes." She talked to them about having a special place, a place where a kid could feel comfortable. She asked them to make that special place in the diorama box.

Jeremy thought about this for a while. He remembered a special place in the woods behind his house where he had made a fort. It was cool and damp there in the summer. It was where he had found his first stick bug, and a great place for collecting lightning bugs. Oh, it felt good to remember.

As he began making the diorama of his fort in the woods, Jeremy thought that when he went home today he might go out there again, and maybe he would find another stick bug or at least some lightning bugs.

Just as he was gluing on the last leaf in his diorama box, the lunch bell sounded. Jeremy was starving! He hadn't felt so hungry in a long time. He ate three hot dogs, a hamburger, and two helpings of macaroni salad. And then, four slices of watermelon. Boy, was his brother wrong about camp food. Camp food tasted terrific. Curiously, no one stopped him from having seconds or thirds or even fourths!

A little while after lunch he and Davey swam in the pool together, and then went off to work on their idea for Bill's Talent Show.

During small group time, the kids talked about how things had changed in their families since the death of the person they loved. Jeremy thought of his smelly camp shirt, and all the other things he forgot to remember, and Dad's cooking, and the mystery lunches that Dad packed for school. His brother was the one who helped him with homework now, and if he forgot to feed Shazaam, no one reminded him except Shazaam, who had taken to howling in the middle of the night. Boy, had life changed. . . .

That evening at home, Jeremy gave Tommy the bright red alligator key chain. Later, the boys walked over to Jeremy's fort in the woods. Tommy said, "Remember last summer when Mom helped us collect all those lightning bugs, and you kept them in your room for a week?" Jeremy's heart started to pound. He looked up at his brother with tears in his eyes. Tommy had some tears too. Tommy put his arm around Jeremy and said, "Let's see how many bugs we can find together - I bet Mom would like that."

It was really dark outside when their dad called them in for bed. They counted thirty-seven lightning bugs in their jar. The bugs sparkled at all different times. Shazaam came right up to the jar in Jeremy's hand. He was curious about those bugs. Little lights going on and off in the dark.

Inside the house, Jeremy held the jar up to show it to his dad. Dad looked carefully and then said, "Jeremy, for camp tomorrow you've been asked to bring in something special, a picture or something to share with the others, a special memory about Mom. Do you have any ideas?"

Jeremy looked at his jar of lighting bugs and smiled. He said, "I think I have it, Dad!"

An unusual thing happened on Thursday. In small group, Davey pulled out a photograph of a man standing next to a smaller version of Davey on a bike, and handed it to Jeremy. "That's my Dad and me," he said quietly. Jeremy held the picture carefully, looking at it for some time, and then passed it around to the rest of the group. Davey continued, "He died in the World Trade Center." A tear slowly trickled down his cheek.

All the kids were quiet as they gently held Davey's picture, then passed it back to him. No one mentioned a word about Davey speaking at last. One of the children said, "Well then, your dad is a hero."

Jeremy looked at Davey and handed him his jar of lightning bugs. Jeremy told the group about collecting bugs with his mom before she got so sick. And how he had thought that somehow maybe the bugs had made her sick. Now he knew it wasn't the bugs, but something called cancer.

Sue pulled out a raggedy stuffed dog and said, "My Grandma gave me this when I was just a baby. It was the first toy she ever brought me." Jeremy held it in his hands and then passed it to Davey. Again, the kids passed the dog around to each other and gently handed it back to Sue.

As each child shared a special memory, Jeremy began to feel that he did have friends after all - friends who could understand, especially Davey. Jeremy had learned Davey's secret, and was glad he now understood the message of Davey's taped-

together heart. He learned that when kids have very sad feelings they need someone to be with them, someone to listen so they can start to talk about their feelings.

At the end of group everyone was smiling. Sue started to sing the camp song. And though Brad, Davey, and Jeremy made faces and groaned, soon they were singing too, as they joined the circle of campers at the end of the day -

"I know a place called Camp Good Grief -
It's a place where friends abound . . ."

Friday was the best day of camp. Tommy and Dad were coming with Jeremy today. Jeremy couldn't wait to show his dad all the things he'd made in arts and crafts, and then take Dad and Tommy to see his art therapy projects. Of course he and Davey had their big surprise for the Talent Show.

While Dad went with the therapists, Jeremy took Tommy to meet all the kids at camp, and Katie and Bill too, and then to dance and sing with a D.J. called Terry Tunes.

After lunch Dad, Tommy, and Jeremy went to small group. Linda, the art therapist, joined them to tell a story about taking an imaginary journey under the sea. In the story a boy swam under the sea into a cave. At the end of the cave he saw some sunbeams, and he swam toward them. The sunbeams lit up a small island that was lush and green. The island reminded Jeremy of Camp Good Grief.

Linda suggested they all might find a gift on their imaginary island. Then she asked them to make their gift out of Model Magic. Jeremy and Tommy got right to work. Jeremy's dad seemed to have trouble getting started, but soon joined in. Jeremy was surprised to see what his dad made. It was a treasure box full of hearts! Jeremy laughed, "We *are* on an island. Maybe we're on *Treasure* Island!"

Just as they finished, Bill blew the whistle. The Talent Show was about to begin. Davey and Jeremy were the second act. They both felt a little nervous. Jeremy was wondering if he and Davey could really do this. When it was their turn, there was Anne sitting in the front row cheering for them. Tommy and Dad were standing nearby, watching and smiling, and so were Katie, Brad, Sue, Linda, and Peggy. . . .

Jeremy tapped his magic wand on Davey's baseball cap three times, tap-tap-tap, and exclaimed," Abracadabra!" Jeremy pulled a quarter out of Davey's right ear!

Davey took his magic wand and tapped it on Jeremy's shoulder three times, tap-tap-tap, and in a perfectly clear voice said, "Sup-er-ca-li-frag-i-lis-tic-ex-pi-al-i-do-cious!" Then he pulled a small rubber snake from Jeremy's shorts pocket. The whole camp began to clap, and there were lots and lots of cheers! Jeremy and Davey took a bow. Jeremy found himself smiling from ear to ear, just like everyone else.

When Jeremy went up to his dad after the show he said, "Dad, do you think I could come back to Camp Good Grief next year?" Jeremy's dad smiled the best smile Jeremy had seen in a long time! . . .

The Camp Good Grief Song

Words and music by Christine B. Rannie Grimbol
(Pastoral Care Coordinator, East End Hospice, 1995-2000)

I am fine at Camp Good Grief,
I am fine all day.
I am fine if I'm laughin' or I'm cryin' -
I know I'm fine at Camp Good Grief.

Oh yes! Let's hold hands together
And sing a song of friends and games.
Oh yes! Let's hold hands together
And be glad for the love in each of our names . . .

I know a place called Camp Good Grief,
It's a place where friends abound.
I know a place called Camp Good Grief,
It's a place where hope is found

Oh yes! Let's hold hands together
And sing a song of friends and games.
Oh yes! Let's hold hands together
And be glad for the love in each of our names . . .

I'm so fine at Camp Good Grief,
I'm so fine all day.
I'm so fine if I'm laughin' or I'm cryin'-
I'm so fine at Camp Good Grief,
I'm so fine at Camp Good Grief,
I'm so fine at Camp…Good…Grief!

My Friends

_____

_____

_____

_____

_____

_____

_____

_____

_____

_____

_____

_____

_____

_____

_____

From Our Kids & Parents

From Kids –

"When I'm older I'd like to help the kids at Camp Good Grief."

"What I really like about the camp is that I got to be with other kids who have lost someone too, and I got to talk about it and everyone understood."

"I'm not the only one who lost a parent."

From Parents –

"Camp Good Grief made her happy, and then she could talk about her sister and how much she missed her – and she was understood by everyone."

"It made my sons aware that they are not alone."

"Camp made him feel more comfortable with himself and it seems as though he fits into the world again."

"She hasn't cried herself to sleep about her father since camp."

"I think it helped him feel he was not alone in his loss, that other children have lost a parent."

"I love that my children were so comfortable and happy there. I haven't seen them consistently happy in a long time."

"She is able to explain her feelings and now realizes that it is o.k. to cry, and she doesn't hide her emotions from me."

"I believe it gave him the opportunity to try something out in a safe place and to have success."